5/16

This book belongs to

WITHDRAWN

CHECK BACK OF BOOK ON RETURN.

Heather Hill

Sundown Hill

Crystal Cave

Golden Meadow

Moonshine Pond

Dewdrop Spring

Honeydew Meadow

Mulberry Bushes

Misty Wood Rabbit Warren

HOME SWEET HOME

How many *Fairy Animals* books have you collected?

- Chloe the Kitten
- Bella the Bunny
- Paddy the Puppy
- Mia the Mouse
- Hailey the Hedgehog
- Sophie the Squirrel
- Poppy the Pony
- Betsy the Bunny
- Daisy the Deer
- Katie the Kitten
- Polly the Puppy
- Paige the Pony

Fairy Animals

of Misty Wood

Polly the Puppy

Lily Small

EGMONT

With special thanks to Anne Marie Ryan.

EGMONT
We bring stories to life

Polly the Puppy first published in Great Britain 2015
by Egmont UK Limited
The Yellow Building, 1 Nicholas Road
London W11 4AN

Text copyright © 2015 Hothouse Fiction Ltd
Illustrations copyright © 2015 Kirsteen Harris Jones

ISBN 978 1 4052 7664 1

www.egmont.co.uk
www.hothousefiction.com
www.fairyanimals.com

A CIP catalogue record for this title is available from the British Library.

Printed and bound in Great Britain by The CPI Group

59590/1

MIX
Paper
FSC FSC® C018306

Contents

CHAPTER ONE

School Bells

Polly the Puppy *loved* going to school. She loved playing with her friends. She loved her teacher, Miss Pammy. And she loved learning how to be a good little Pollen Puppy.

There was just one problem. The Fairy Animals of Misty Wood went to school outdoors. And on sunny spring mornings, there was no place in the world more glorious than Misty Wood.

There were flowers blooming all around, trees rustling in the breeze, and the sky was always a brilliant shade of sapphire blue. There were so many beautiful things to gaze at that it was hard

for Polly to concentrate on her lessons!

Today, the young Pollen Puppies were having a lesson in Bluebell Glade. Polly looked around at the carpet of violet blossoms swaying in the warm breeze. She sniffed deeply as their sweet perfume wafted over her, blending with the fresh, earthy smell of Misty Wood. *Mmm* – it was lovely!

POLLY THE PUPPY

Polly closed her big, chocolatey-brown eyes for a moment. She imagined herself rolling around and around in the flowers, until her golden fur was covered in their scent.

A gentle voice interrupted her daydream. 'Didn't you get enough sleep last night, Polly?' asked Miss Pammy.

Polly's eyes flew open wide. *Oops!* Her teacher had caught her

daydreaming again.

'N-no, Miss,' said Polly. 'I mean, yes.' She sighed dreamily and tried to explain. 'It's just that the bluebells are so pretty and sweet-smelling. I was wondering what it would be like to roll around in them.'

'The bluebells are beautiful, Polly,' Miss Pammy said kindly. 'But today's lesson is very important, so please pay attention.'

Then Miss Pammy turned back to the rest of the class. 'As you know, all the fairy animals in Misty Wood have important jobs to do,' she said. 'We are Pollen Puppies, so we flick our tails to send pollen into the air. Can anyone tell me why?'

Polly's friend Perry, a perky little puppy with brown and white patches, flapped his sparkling wings frantically.

'To make more flowers grow, Miss!' he answered eagerly.

Miss Pammy smiled. 'That's correct, Perry.'

Polly sighed. She wished she could be clever like Perry. He never seemed to get distracted.

'But it's important to only flick *five* flowers at a time,' Miss Pammy said. 'Otherwise you will fill the air with too much pollen.' Gazing around at the eager

puppies, she asked, 'Does anyone know why we don't want too much pollen in the air?'

Once again, Perry knew the answer. He bounced up and down, wagging his tail furiously until Miss Pammy chose him. 'Because it will make other fairy animals sneeze, Miss!' he said.

Fluttering over to a cluster of bluebells, Miss Pammy showed the class what to do.

Everyone counted along as she wagged her fluffy tail over five stems of bluebells. Every time her tail swished over a flower, a little cloud of pollen floated into the air.

'Now it's your turn,' Miss Pammy told the class. 'I want you to spread out and practise counting to five.'

Bluebell Glade was suddenly filled with a flurry of sparkling wings. They sparkled like jewels in the sunlight as Pollen Puppies flew around, looking for a good spot to practise counting.

Polly landed softly among a cluster of bluebells. Nearby, Perry

was already hard at work. His brown tail flicked back and forth as he loudly counted to five.

Determined to show her teacher that she had been paying attention, Polly brushed her tail over one flower.

'ONE,' she said loudly, as a puff of pollen rose into the air.

'TWO,' she said, carefully wagging her tail over another graceful stem of bluebells.

'THREE,' she said, sweeping her tail over a third stem.

Polly took a deep breath, enjoying the delicious scent of the bluebells. Then she shook her head and forced herself to concentrate. She didn't want to make a mistake.

What comes after three? she asked herself.

As she tried to remember, Polly peered down at the delicate bluey-purple flower by her paws.

With their curling petals, the dainty blossoms really did look like tiny bells.

Her ears pricked up with curiosity. Polly wondered what bluebells would sound like if they could make music. She was sure it would be a sweet, chiming sound. Suddenly, Polly imagined a tune played by hundreds of bluebells tinkling on the breeze.

The song was so lively that

Polly couldn't resist dancing.
Fluttering her glittering wings and
swishing her tail back and forth to
the rhythm, Polly danced around
Bluebell Glade to the imaginary
sound of a bluebell band.

'*La, di-da, la-la,*' she sang
happily, under her breath. '*La-la-la –*'

Suddenly, a very loud noise
interrupted the music in Polly's
head.

'Ahhhhhh-CHOOOOO!'

It was Chloe the Cobweb Kitten, flying back from her morning duty of decorating cobwebs with sparkling dewdrops. Her pretty eyes were streaming, and her pink nose twitched as she sneezed again and again.

Polly looked up in dismay. All around her was a huge cloud of pollen, drifting into the sky. She'd lost count of how many bluebells she was flicking!

'I'm so sorry!' Polly called
to Chloe. But the Cobweb Kitten
couldn't reply. She sneezed and
spluttered as she tried to get away
from the pollen.

Miss Pammy hurried over. 'Polly! How many bluebells did you flick?'

Polly hung her head. 'I'm not sure, Miss. I counted to three, but then I started thinking about bluebells making music and . . . er . . . I lost count.'

'It's lovely that you have such a big imagination, Polly,' sighed Miss Pammy. 'But being a Pollen Puppy is a very important job.

And to do it properly, you need to be able to count.'

'I'm sorry, Miss,' Polly said, her eyes brimming with tears.

'Let's try again,' her teacher said gently. 'You said you flicked three bluebells. So if you flicked two more, how many bluebells would that make altogether?'

'Er . . . four?' Polly guessed.

Miss Pammy shook her head sadly. 'No, dear.'

Perry bounded over. 'The answer's five!' he barked.

As usual, Perry was right.

'I'm never going to be a good Pollen Puppy,' Polly whimpered, her pink wings drooping.

Her teacher patted her with a soft paw. 'Of course you will,' she said. 'You just need to concentrate harder on your schoolwork, and practise your counting. Can you try that for me?'

Polly's wings perked up again.

'I will,' she promised, nodding so hard that her ears flapped. 'I'm going to learn how to count to five *today*, and by tomorrow I'll be perfect at it!'

Polly was determined to be a good Pollen Puppy, and make Miss Pammy proud. She would learn how to count to five – even if it meant never daydreaming again!

CHAPTER TWO

Tea for Two

For the rest of the lesson, Polly

listened carefully as her teacher

explained how to tell when bluebells

were ready to make pollen.

Her attention didn't wander once,

even when a nearby bird chirped a beautiful song. Nor when she saw a pretty blue beetle scuttle by, so shiny that it looked like a gem.

Before long, Miss Pammy announced that it was time to go home. The frisky Pollen Puppies yipped joyfully, and frolicked around Bluebell Glade.

'Remember,' Miss Pammy called after the playful puppies, 'only five flowers at a time!'

24

Perry dashed over to Polly. 'We're going to play sliding down the rainbow,' he said, wagging his tail excitedly. 'Want to come?'

'I can't,' Polly said reluctantly. 'I need to learn how to count.'

Polly *loved* sliding down the rainbow with her friends. It was one of her favourite things to do. But she had promised Miss Pammy that she would practise counting.

POLLY THE PUPPY

'You can count the colours of
the rainbow,' Perry suggested. He
pointed a paw at the enormous
rainbow that shimmered in the
sky above Misty Wood. 'It's easy
– there are seven colours.' Then
Perry rattled them off. 'Red,
orange, yellow, green, blue,
indigo and violet!'

Polly tried to count the
beautiful bands of colour sparkling
in the sunlight. 'One . . . two . . .

three,' she counted slowly.

But before she'd even counted half the colours, she was picturing herself whooshing down the rainbow at top speed.

'I'm sorry, Perry,' she said sadly. 'Rainbows are just too much fun. I need to find something really *boring* to count.'

'OK,' Perry said. 'Good luck!' Waving goodbye with his paw, he flew into the air and caught up

28

with a group of Pollen Puppies
heading towards the rainbow slide.

Polly heaved a sigh. She
wished she could join her friends.
But she wished even more that she
could be a good Pollen Puppy –
and to do that, she needed to know
how to count to five.

Fluttering her wings, Polly
rose into the sky. Below her, Misty
Wood spread out in a sea of
colour. Beyond the violet carpet

of Bluebell Glade, Dandelion
Dell glowed with hundreds of
golden dandelions bobbing in the
sunshine.

The silvery waters of
Moonshine Pond sparkled
invitingly and Honeydew Meadow
was a vibrant emerald green,
dotted with white daisies. In the
very heart of Misty Wood was
a cluster of ancient trees. Polly
decided to head there first.

★

Polly landed in a clearing, surrounded by mighty oak trees. Their glossy green leaves rustled in the breeze. She thought it sounded like they were whispering. What secrets could the oak trees be telling each other, she wondered?

Maybe they're talking about the secret to becoming so tall, she thought with a smile, *or how to grow so many leaves.*

But then she caught herself

starting to daydream and shook

her head sternly. *Focus, Polly!*

Polly put her little nose to

the ground and started sniffing. She padded about the clearing, looking for something boring to count. It wasn't easy, as everything in Misty Wood was so interesting!

At the base of a tall tree with a gnarled trunk, Polly found a hollow lined with soft moss. She felt around inside it with her paw and discovered a stash of acorns.

Acorns aren't very interesting,

thought Polly. *They're perfect for practising counting.*

Taking a deep breath, Polly began to count. She picked the acorns up one at a time and carefully lined them up in a row. 'One . . . two . . .'

But when Polly picked up the third acorn, its cap fell off. Holding the little cap in her paw, Polly peered at it closely.

It looks like a hat made for a

teeny tiny elf, she thought with a giggle. She turned it over. Now it looked like a dainty little cup.

Polly suddenly imagined herself at a tea party. All the guests were fairy animals, looking their very best! Their wings glittered, their fur gleamed, and beautiful flower garlands sparkled around their necks.

'Do have some rosehip tea, dear,' Polly said, pretending to be

a host offering tea to her guests.

'Why thank you,' Polly replied in her poshest voice. 'How kind of you to offer, Madame Rosehip Blossom.' She lifted the tiny acorn cap to her mouth and pretended to sip from it. She could practically taste the sweet rosehip tea.

'My name isn't Madame Rosehip Blossom,' someone said crossly, making Polly jump. 'And I *didn't* offer you my acorns.'

Polly swirled around and saw a Stardust Squirrel staring at her suspiciously.

'Oh, no, I wasn't eating your acorns,' Polly explained. 'I was just pretending to drink from them.'

She showed him the acorn cap.
'See? It looks like a cute little cup.'

The Stardust Squirrel squinted at the acorn cap. 'Oh. They *do* look like little cups!' He smiled at Polly. 'My name's Sammy, by the way.'

'I'm Polly. Do you want to have a fairy tea-party with me?' Polly asked her new friend. Sammy nodded eagerly.

'That can be our table,' Polly said, pointing to an old tree stump. 'Let's make it look pretty enough for a fairy party!'

Sammy set the tree-stump table with acorn caps. Polly picked a small bunch of violets and arranged them in the middle.

'It looks lovely,' Polly said happily.

'Wait, something's missing,' Sammy said. He twirled round,

giving his tail a shake, and suddenly the whole table was sparkling. The Stardust Squirrels' special job was to sprinkle Misty Wood with stardust from their big bushy tails. Now the clearing looked even more beautiful!

'I'll be Madame Rosehip Blossom,' Polly said, picking up a twig and pretending it was a magic wand. 'Can I offer you some delicious rosehip tea?'

Sammy giggled. 'If it's all right with you, Madame Rosehip Blossom, I'd rather *eat* the acorns!'

So Sammy munched on acorns, while Polly sipped cup after cup of pretend rosehip tea.

'What lovely weather we've been having,' Polly said, glancing at the sunlight streaming through the branches overhead. She hoped this was the sort of thing you talked about at tea parties.

Sammy just nodded. His cheeks were too full of nuts to speak!

Suddenly, a voice from up in a tree called out, 'Sammy! Where are you?'

Sammy sprang to his feet.
'Oh no! My mum told me to bring
five acorns home for lunch. I've
got to go! It's been really fun
playing with you, Polly – let's
play again soon.'

Sammy waved goodbye to
Polly, and then quickly gathered
up five acorns. He scampered
up a nearby tree, leaving a
trail of shimmering stardust
behind him.

When Polly heard Sammy say 'five', she suddenly remembered what she'd come into the woods to do.

'Oh dear,' she said, looking around the clearing. She was *supposed* to be practising counting – not having a fairy tea-party with a new friend! Who knew that acorns were so interesting?

The warm sun was shining high above Misty Woods,

44

so there was still plenty of time to find something else to count. Something really boring, that wouldn't make her want to daydream or play. Polly just needed to find it!

CHAPTER THREE

Princess Polly

Polly fluttered her wings and flew
high into the air. As she left the
trees behind, her big brown eyes
scanned the ground, searching for
something to count.

Far below, Honeydew Meadow rippled in the breeze like a sea of green. But what were all those little white spots?

Polly let out a yelp of excitement. Daisies! There were lots and lots of them, so they'd be just right to practise counting on.

She landed right in the middle of the meadow and bounded around, picking daisies until she had a big bunch to count.

Right, she thought firmly. *This time I won't let anything distract me!*

'One,' she said, picking up a daisy and setting it aside. 'Two,' she counted, carefully placing a second daisy next to the first one.

'Three,' she said, putting another flower in the row.

I'm counting! Polly thought proudly. She stopped for a moment to admire how pretty the flowers looked, lined up in a row.

Polly thought that the daisies' snowy-white petals looked like little crowns around their yellow heads. And that gave Polly a brilliant idea. Daisies weren't just good for counting – they were also perfect for making crowns!

Picking up two daisies, Polly wove their delicate stems together. Then she added another, and another, until she had a long chain of daisies. She joined the two ends

together to make a circle and placed the crown on top of her head.

Polly stood on her hind legs and pranced around the meadow. 'I am Princess Polly, ruler of Honeydew Meadow!' she barked at the flowers around her. 'I am in charge of everyone, and you all have to do whatever I say!'

'Oh no, I don't,' said a soft voice.

Startled, Polly
dropped down
to all fours and
spun around to
see a silvery Bud

Bunny. The bunny's soft whiskers
trembled as she stared at Polly.

'Oh, hello,' Polly said, hoping
she hadn't upset the bunny. 'I'm
Polly. I was just playing at being
a princess. I was bossing around
the daisies, not you!'

The Bud Bunny giggled, making her fluffy tail shake. '*Phew!*' she said. 'Can I play too?'

Polly wagged her tail in delight. Games were always much more fun if you had a friend to play with. 'Of course! What's your name?' she asked the Bud Bunny.

'Bella,' the bunny replied.

'Come on then, Princess Bella,' Polly said. 'We need to make you a crown!'

Polly and Bella dashed around
the meadow, picking more daisies.

Whenever they came across
a flower that hadn't opened
yet, Bella nudged the bud with

her velvety nose and the petals
unfurled as if by magic.

It was the Bud Bunnies' job to
make flowers blossom, and Polly
loved watching it happen.

When they'd gathered big
bunches of daisies, Polly and Bella
sat down in the sunshine and wove
the stems together with their paws.
But they didn't stop when they'd
finished making Bella's crown.
They made daisy collars for each

other, too, and pretty daisy cuffs
to go around their paws.

Polly thought that she and
her new friend looked very grand.
'Let's have a princess parade!' she
exclaimed.

'Good idea,' cried Bella. 'We
can greet all of our loyal subjects!'

Polly scampered across the
meadow, with Bella hopping along
behind her. The two princesses
waved to a pair of bright orange

butterflies that were flitting from flower to flower.

'Good day, beautiful butterflies,' Princess Polly shouted in her grandest voice.

'Oh, you sound very royal,' Bella whispered, giggling.

They waved to a Dream Deer grazing on the meadow, and a snail inching up a blade of grass.

'Greetings, loyal subjects of Honeydew Kingdom,' Polly

called, while Princess Bella nodded regally to everyone they passed.

They waved to the bees buzzing back to their hive, to the robins building a nest, and to a spider busy spinning a web.

After parading around the whole meadow, Polly and Bella were tired. 'These can be our thrones!' Polly panted, flopping down onto a big rock. Bella sat on a rock next to Polly's.

Perched on their rock thrones, the two pretend princesses looked out over the meadow.

'Honeydew Meadow is the most beautiful kingdom in the world,' Polly murmured, and Bella bobbed her head in agreement.

As they rested, they listened to the soothing sounds of the meadow. Hidden by the long grass, crickets chirped like an orchestra of tiny violins, and birds

POLLY THE PUPPY

in the cloudless sky tweeted along.

It made Polly want to dance.

'Let's have a royal ball!'
exclaimed Polly, leaping off her
throne.

She and Bella joined paws
and danced around and around
to the sweet meadow music. When
they were too dizzy to dance
anymore, they collapsed, laughing,
in a heap on the grass.

'It's been really fun playing

princesses with you, Polly,' Bella
said when she'd caught her breath.
'But now I have to get back to the
rabbit warren. I promised my three
little brothers that I would tell
them a story.'

As soon as she heard the word
'three', Polly remembered that
it was the last number she had
counted.

Oh no! Once again, she'd got
distracted before she could finish

counting. How was she going to be a good Pollen Puppy if she never learnt to count to five?

Nuzzling noses with her new friend, and promising to play princesses again soon, Polly hurried off. Playing with Bella had been really fun – but now it was time to get serious about counting!

CHAPTER FOUR
Smooth Sailing

Polly wandered out of Honeydew

Meadow, and scratched her ear

thoughtfully. Where could she find

something really, *really* boring to

count? Acorns and daisies had

been much too interesting.

Polly gazed around, looking for inspiration . . .

A short distance away, she spied a Bark Badger carving designs on a tree trunk with his sharp claws. Bark Badgers decorated the trunks of the Misty Wood trees with beautiful patterns. They were known to be kind, clever creatures. Polly hoped he might be able to give her some advice.

'Hello,' she called, fluttering over to the Bark Badger. 'I'm Polly. I was wondering if you could help me – I'm trying to learn how to count.'

The badger peered down his long black-and-white snout at Polly. 'Why, of course,' he said, nodding wisely. 'I'm Bobby. And I'm happy to help you – counting is a very important skill for every young fairy animal to learn.'

Swiping his claws over the tree's bark, Bobby drew a swirly shape. 'One,' he said in his deep, rumbly voice. 'Two.' As he counted, he drew more whirly

67

shapes on the tree trunk.

But Polly was struggling to pay attention to the numbers the badger was saying. Instead, her eyes were drawn to the patterns Bobby was making. They reminded her of snail shells. And *this* made her think of how much fun it would be to be a snail.

Imagine carrying your house around on your back! she thought to herself. *Maybe I'll play at being a*

68

snail. I could make my very own shell
out of tree bark, and . . . Oops!

She'd done it again!

'It's no use,' Polly said aloud,
shaking her head. 'Thank you for
trying to help me, Bobby, but your
lovely swirly carvings are far too
interesting for me to count. I need
to find something really boring to
practise on.'

'Hmm,' said Bobby, and
scratched his head. A leaf floated

down from the branches above, onto the ground in front of them. Bobby picked it up and handed it to Polly. 'How about leaves?' he suggested. 'They aren't *nearly* as interesting as bark.'

It was a wonderful idea.
'Thank you, Bobby!' Polly
exclaimed. Then she dashed off to
find more leaves to count.

She collected an oval-shaped
leaf from a tall beech tree,
a glossy, heart-shaped leaf from
a sweet-smelling lilac tree, and a
great, big leaf with rough edges
from a chestnut tree. Soon she had
more leaves than she could carry,
so she laid them all out on the

bank of Moonshine Pond.

It's amazing how many different shapes and colours and sizes of leaf there are, thought Polly. But she refused to get distracted by how the leaves looked.

Polly began to count. 'One . . . two . . . three . . .'

But when she got to the fourth leaf, a gust of wind lifted it up into the air. The leaf spun for a moment, twirling on the breeze

like a dancer. Then it landed
lightly on the shimmering water of
Moonshine Pond.

Polly watched as the leaf
started to drift across the pond's
rippling surface. It was just like
a little boat. She thought the leaf
looked a bit sad, all alone on the
water. It needed some company.

Polly waded into the cool,
clear water and floated another
leaf on the water's surface.

She gave the leaf a gentle push with her nose, and it sailed off on the breeze.

Suddenly, Polly had a brilliant idea. The leaf boats could have a race! She splashed out of the water and gathered up more of her leaves. Setting them on the water, she watched as they sailed away. At first, an elm leaf was in the lead – but then the big chestnut leaf quickly gained on it!

One of the leaf boats crashed into a lilypad and sank under the surface, and another leaf got nibbled by a fish, but the rest of Polly's boats sailed proudly across the water.

Polly jumped up and down with excitement, wagging her tail wildly. 'Faster! Faster!' she cried, cheering the leaf boats on.

'I'm going as fast as I can,' a little voice squeaked.

'Wow! Talking leaf-boats!' Polly exclaimed. Even in her wildest daydreams she wouldn't have imagined *talking* leaf-boats.

'First you shout at me to go faster, then you call me a talking

76

leaf-boat!' the
little voice said
crossly.

Polly turned
round to see a tiny brown Moss
Mouse down by the water.

Moss Mice did a very
important job. They shaped
velvety moss into soft cushions
so that the fairy animals of Misty
Woods would have cosy beds
to sleep on.

This Moss Mouse was busy gathering moss from the rocks along the water's edge.

'Oh dear,' Polly said with a laugh, 'I wasn't shouting at you – I was cheering my leaf boats on.'

'What leaf boats?' the mouse asked. Curious, she scurried over to where Polly stood.

'They're having a race!' Polly explained, pointing at the boats.

78

SMOOTH SAILING

They were sailing swiftly towards the other side of the pond.

'I wonder which one will win?' murmured the mouse.

'There's only one way to find out,' Polly said. 'Want to come with me?'

The mouse nodded eagerly. 'I'm Marnie,' she said.

'Nice to meet you. I'm Polly.' Crouching down, she added, 'Hop on my back and I'll give you a ride!'

Marnie squeaked excitedly
and climbed onto Polly's back. She
clung to her fur with tiny paws.

As Polly scampered around
the edge of the pond, Marnie
told her everything that was
happening.

'Ooh! The oak leaf is over-taking,' Marnie squeaked. 'But the elm leaf's close behind.'

Running as fast as she could, Polly let out little yips and yaps of encouragement to urge the leaf boats on.

A sudden gust of wind made all the leaves pick up speed as they skimmed across the pond.

'Now the lilac leaf is in the lead,' announced Marnie.

'But who will make it across first?'

Polly finally got to the other side of the pond and skidded to a stop. Marnie hopped off her back and the two new friends watched the end of the race together.

'We have a winner!' panted Polly, splashing into the water to retrieve the lilac leaf.

Padding out of the water, she shook herself all over, spraying drops of water everywhere.

Marnie laughed. 'Well, when I came out to do my job today, I certainly I wasn't counting on seeing a boat race – or getting soaking wet,' she said, brushing shiny drops of water off her fur.

'Oh no!' Polly groaned as soon as she heard the word 'counting'. She'd done it *again*. She was meant to be counting the leaves, not racing them against each other.

Polly looked up in dismay.
The afternoon sun was beginning
to dip low in the sky, which glowed
with pink and purple streaks.

The trees around the pond were casting long shadows across the water's surface.

Polly's heart sank. She'd promised Miss Pammy that she'd learn how to count today – but there was hardly any time left to do it!

CHAPTER FIVE

Sweet Dreams

'What's wrong?' Marnie asked
Polly.

The puppy flopped down on
the ground and covered her eyes
with her paws. 'I promised my

teacher that I'd learn how to count to five today, but I keep getting distracted. I was supposed to be counting the leaves, but I turned them into boats and now they're gone,' she whimpered. 'And if I can't count, I'll never be a good Pollen Puppy.' Tears glistened in Polly's dark eyes.

'Don't get upset,' Marnie said, hopping on to Polly's head and patting it comfortingly. 'I know

just the thing for you to count . . .'

Polly took her paws off her eyes and watched hopefully as Marnie scuttled to and fro, her pink tail dragging behind her.

First, the little mouse scurried over to a huge weeping willow tree by the banks of Moonshine Pond. She scooped up piles of moss from around its thick trunk with her nimble paws. Then, she darted over to the damp rocks by

89

the water's edge and gathered up
more dark-green moss.

Returning to Polly, Marnie
patted the moss she'd gathered
into five little cushions.

'Ta-da!' she cried, sounding
pleased with herself. 'Now you can
count these!'

Polly ran her paw over the
soft, velvety moss cushions. 'Thank
you so much,' she said gratefully.
'But I'm just not sure I can do it.'

SWEET DREAMS

'Don't be silly,' Marnie told Polly firmly, dabbing the puppy's tears with a bit of moss. 'I *know* you can be a brilliant Pollen Puppy. Just think of how clever you were to come up with the idea for the leaf-boat race. Now you just need to focus all of that cleverness on counting.'

Polly suddenly felt a lot more cheerful. Her new friend was so helpful. 'Thanks, Marnie.'

The Moss Mouse looked up at the orange sky. The moon was just starting to peek out from behind a tree. 'I'd better go. I promised my mum I'd be back home before dark. Good luck, Polly. You can do it!'

Marnie kissed Polly on her glossy black nose, then fluttered her sparkly pink wings and rose into the air. As she headed home, Polly thought she looked like a shooting star, twinkling in the twilight.

Polly glanced down at the moss cushions and remembered what Marnie had told her.

She needed to use every bit of cleverness she had to count.

Polly stroked the first moss cushion. 'One,' she said with determination.

'Two,' she said, moving the second cushion alongside the first.

The moss felt so soft and springy. Polly wondered what it

would be like to bounce up and down on it . . . up and down and round and round . . . No! She wasn't going to get distracted – she was going to focus.

'Three,' she counted, pushing the third cushion next to the others, and then . . . 'Four.'

Polly yawned. Counting was so exhausting! Lined up next to each other, the moss cushions looked like one big, comfy pillow.

The sort of pillow that was just the size for a tired Pollen Puppy . . .

It wouldn't hurt to have a little rest, would it? After all, it was very hard to concentrate if you were feeling sleepy.

Polly climbed onto the moss cushion and curled up, tucking her tail beneath her. She let out a little growl of contentment. The moss was smooth and soft, and even more comfortable than she had

imagined. It felt like the cushion was giving her a warm, cosy cuddle!

Polly nestled deeper into the moss. She'd had such a busy day.

Maybe she'd just close her eyes for a moment . . .

Before she knew it, Polly was sound asleep!

★

As she slept, Polly had an amazing dream. She was having a royal tea-party in the Heart of Misty Wood, and all her new friends were there.

'Hello, Princess Polly,' called Sammy the Stardust Squirrel,

scattering sparkling stardust around the clearing as he scampered over to her. 'I brought you some acorns.'

Bella the Bud Bunny hopped over to Polly and nuzzled her nose. 'I made this for you, Princess Polly,' she said, placing a daisy crown on Polly's head.

Bobby the Bark Badger was busy carving beautiful swirling patterns on the trunks of the oak

trees surrounding the clearing. 'It wouldn't be a party without decorations,' he said, chuckling.

'We can all sit on these!' Marnie the Moss Mouse cried, shaping soft moss cushions for Polly's guests to sit on.

In her dream, everyone sat down around a tree stump table and nibbled juicy berries, ripe plums and sweet nuts drizzled with honey.

As Princess Polly and her
friends sipped rosehip tea from
acorn caps, a leaf floated down
from one of the trees.

'Everyone find a leaf,' cried
Princess Polly. 'We're going to
have a boat race!'

In a flash, all the fairy
animals were flying through
the air to Moonshine Pond.
When they landed by the pond,
the leaves they were holding grew

bigger and bigger and bigger –

until they were just the right size

for Polly and her friends to sail on!

'First one to the other side

is the winner!' exclaimed Polly,

hopping onto a glossy oak leaf.

Polly's silky ears blew back

in the breeze as her boat sailed

smoothly across the pond.

Fluttering her wings as fast as she

could, Polly yipped in excitement

as her boat took the lead!

But just before she reached the other side of the pond, Polly's leaf boat suddenly started to shake. And as the boat started to shake, Polly started to wobble. And as she started to wobble she could feel herself nearly slide off the leaf – and into the water! But just before Polly plunged into the water, she woke up with a start.

Something – or someone – *was* shaking her! But it was too dark

104

to see who it was. The sun had set long ago and the sky was now an inky black.

Polly's golden fur stood on end. She was afraid of the dark – especially when she was out in it all by herself! Her lovely dream had become a nightmare.

Then she noticed a pale, ghostly light hovering above her. Polly felt even more scared. 'Wh-who are you?' she stammered.

CHAPTER SIX

Five New Friends

'Don't be frightened,' said a kind voice. 'It's only me – Maisie.'

The light moved closer and Polly realised that it was a net filled with glowing moonbeams.

FIVE NEW FRIENDS

As it came even nearer, she saw
that it was held in the pink claws
of a Moonbeam Mole. The mole
squinted down her long snout at
Polly.

'I was out collecting moonbeams and heard you yelping
in your sleep,' explained Maisie,
sounding concerned. 'I thought
you were having a bad dream so
I woke you up.'

'It was actually a wonderful

dream, in the beginning,' Polly said, her tail drooping. 'But I shouldn't have been dreaming at all!' She buried her face in her paws and moaned, 'Oh dear, oh dear, oh dear, oh dear, oh dear!'

Marnie chuckled softly. 'You just said *oh dear* five times! Can things really be that bad?'

'Yes! And that's just it – everyone can count to five except for me,' Polly said, looking up. 'I promised my teacher I would learn how today, but instead I had a tea party with my new friend Sammy, played princesses with my new friend Bella, watched my new friend Bobby draw bark patterns,

and had a leaf race with my new
friend Marnie. It made me so tired
that I fell fast asleep.'

Then she wailed, 'And I *still*
don't know how to count to five!'

'Hmm,' Maisie said,
drumming her long claws on
Polly's moss cushion. 'It sounds
like you had a lot of fun today.'

Polly sniffed. 'Yes,' she
admitted, 'I did have lots of fun.'
Her tail gave a little twitch of

happiness as she thought about her adventures.

'And you made a lot of new friends today,' Maisie pointed out.

Polly nodded, and her tail started to wag more quickly. 'Oh yes,' she said, 'Sammy, Bella, Bobby and Marnie were all so nice. I was really lucky to make four new friends in just one day.' Her ears perked up as Polly realised what she'd done.

112

'Oh! I just counted something!'

'Yes, you did,' Maisie said
with a smile. 'And would you like
to be my friend, too?'

'Of course!' Polly said.

'Well then,' Maisie said, tilting her head, 'how many friends do you have now?'

Polly's furry brow furrowed as she concentrated hard. 'If I have four friends, and I add one more, I have . . .' She looked up at Maisie and smiled more brightly than the mole's net full of moonbeams. 'I have five friends!'

'Very good,' Maisie exclaimed, clapping in delight. 'So you did

learn to count today, after all!'

Polly couldn't wait to show Perry and Miss Pammy and all her friends at school that she'd learned how to count. She would be a good Pollen Puppy after all! Looking up at the luminous moon, Polly let out a little yelp of happiness. But then her yelp turned into a howl.

'Oh no,' she groaned. 'I may know how to count now, but I

don't know how to find my way
home in the dark.'

'I'll take you,' Maisie offered.
'We can use my net of moonbeams
to light the way.'

'Are you sure?' Polly said.
The Moonbeam Moles worked at
night when the other fairy animals
were fast asleep. It was their job
to gather up moonbeams in their
nets and drop them in Moonshine
Pond so that the water sparkled

and shimmered. Polly didn't want
to get Maisie into trouble.

'Of course,' Maisie replied.
'That's what friends are for!'

Polly and her newest friend
fluttered their wings and rose
into the air. They soared over
Moonshine Pond, which gleamed
in the moonlight. Polly could hear
frogs croaking and owls hooting
in the distance. High above,
stars twinkled like diamonds.

Down below, fireflies danced in the dark like tiny flames.

Polly was surprised to see how beautiful Misty Woods was at night. But then, today had been full of lovely surprises!

★

Even though she'd come home really late, Polly was so excited that she woke before dawn the next morning. She couldn't wait to get to school! After breakfast, she

bounded into Bluebell Glade and greeted Perry with a cheerful bark.

'Sorry you couldn't come sliding down the rainbow yesterday,' Perry said as soon as he saw her. 'It was fun. Did you have a really boring afternoon?'

Polly laughed and shook her head. 'No, it wasn't boring at all. I made lots of new friends!'

Miss Pammy overheard Polly and joined her students. 'Did you

practise your counting as well?'
she asked gently.

'I did,' Polly said, full of pride.
'I made five new friends – Sammy,
Bella, Bobby, Marnie and Maisie.'

As she said each of their
names, Polly brushed her tail over
one bluebell. With each twitch of
her tail, a puff of pollen wafted
into the air. This time, Polly
stopped at five, just as she'd been
taught. She wasn't going to make

anyone sneeze ever again!

Perry cheered, and Miss
Pammy gave Polly a big hug.

'I'm very impressed,' her
teacher said. 'I knew you could do
it!' Then Miss Pammy gave her a
playful look.

'If Perry's your friend too, how
many friends do you have in total,
Polly?'

Perry started to answer, but
Polly held up her paw to stop him.

Perry wasn't the only clever Pollen Puppy now!

'Let me see,' she said thoughtfully. 'Five plus one more equals . . . Six! I have six friends!'

Polly's teacher beamed. 'Excellent work! I'm proud of you.'

'It was easy,' Polly said with a happy bark. 'You can always count on your friends!'

Turn the page for lots of fun Misty Wood activities!

Spot the difference

The picture on the opposite page is slightly different to this one. Can you circle all the differences?

Misty Wood
Word Search

Can you find all these
words from Polly's story?

F	R	I	E	N	D	M	F	L	A	C	O	R	N	I
A	X	E	P	B	L	U	E	B	E	L	L	T	B	N
R	A	I	N	B	O	W	I	B	J	B	E	D	O	V
O	U	Q	S	G	H	Z	A	D	R	E	A	M	A	S
A	P	L	N	C	M	O	S	S	A	N	F	N	T	K

BLUEBELL   RAINBOW   DREAM   LEAF
ACORN   MOSS   BOAT   FRIEND

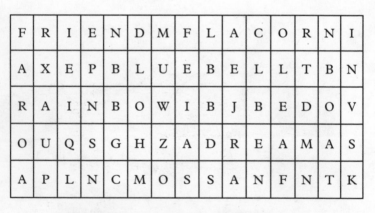